The Alphabets in the garden

By Roger Knights

LITTLE SIMON and colophon are trademarks of Simon & Schuster
Printed in U.S.A.
10 9 8 7 6 5 4 3 2 1
ISBN 0-671-45043-3

D1441242

The Alphabets are very lucky.

They have a lovely big garden where there is always a lot of work to do.

First we must get rid of all these

awful weeds.

That's better!
Now we can plant some seeds.

The Alphabets wonder what sort of flowers will grow.

picks daisies.

picks roses.

picks tulips.

The Alphabets also have a vegetable garden

where they grow
lots of different vegetables.

Today they have picked carrots

and potatoes. Guess what for?

The Alphabets have
a new garden shed
where they keep
all their tools.

Why are they laughing?

Oh dear, an Alphabet
has gotten locked inside.

Who'll let him out?

In the corner
is an old apple
full of juicy red

tree
apples.

Shall we pick some to make
a scrumptious apple pie?

Before we go in, we'll pick some more pretty flowers.

What a lovely day we've had in our garden.

All the Alphabets really enjoy all the lovely things that . . .

there.